Mister Cleghorn's Seal

Mister Cleghorn's Seal

Judith Kerr

HarperCollins *Children's Books*

First published in hardback in Great Britain by HarperCollins *Children's Books* in 2015
First published in paperback in Great Britain by HarperCollins *Children's Books* in 2016
HarperCollins *Children's Books* is a division of HarperCollins*Publishers* Ltd,
1 London Bridge Street, London, SE1 9GF

The HarperCollins website address is: www.harpercollins.co.uk

1 3 5 7 9 10 8 6 4 2

Text and Illustrations © Kerr-Kneale Productions Ltd 2015

ISBN: 978-0-00-818302-8

Judith Kerr asserts the moral right to be identified as
the author and illustrator of this work.

Printed and bound in Spain by Rodesa

MIX
Paper from
responsible sources
FSC C007454

FSC™ is a non-profit international organisation established to promote
the responsible management of the world's forests. Products carrying the
FSC label are independently certified to assure consumers that they come
from forests that are managed to meet the social, economic and
ecological needs of present and future generations,
and other controlled sources.

Find out more about HarperCollins and the environment at
www.harpercollins.co.uk/green

*To my father, who once kept
a seal on his balcony*

Mr Albert Cleghorn was sitting on the balcony outside his flat, watching the sunrise. It was rather a good sunrise, but the pink and orange sky did not cheer him.

Seven o'clock in the morning, he thought. What on earth was he going to do with the whole long day ahead?

Normally at this time Mr Cleghorn was already busy in his shop, sending the paper boy off on his round, laying out the day's editions, and selling them –

along with pipe tobacco and those newfangled cigarettes – to early travellers on their way to the station. Later he'd be rearranging the twelve big jars of different coloured sweets ready for when the children came out of school, and chatting with the local ladies who needed a pencil or a notebook or some brown wrapping paper.

I should never have sold the shop, thought Mr Cleghorn, even though the people who bought it had paid him a tidy sum. *Whatever am I going to do with myself?*

In the street below, things were beginning to stir. The milkman was leading his horse from house to house and the postman – looking up and seeing Mr Cleghorn on his balcony – waved and pointed, to tell him that he had a letter. When Mr Cleghorn went downstairs to fetch it, he found the janitor arguing with a little middle-aged lady. The lady was holding a cage with a small bird in it, and the janitor was shouting, as usual.

"No pets!" shouted the janitor. "You know the rules! No pets in the flats!"

"Oh for goodness' sake," said the lady. "It's only my sister's canary, and I'm looking after it for a few days."

"Well, I shall expect to see it gone by the end of the week," said the janitor and retreated behind the window of his cubbyhole to watch for any further infringements of the rules.

The lady made a funny face at Mr Cleghorn, and he went to pick up his letter. It was from his cousin William. They were having a good summer, wrote William, and what with all the holidaymakers, the fishing business was thriving. So, when was Albert going to come and stay? Included in the letter was a card with a picture of the harbour and the printed words 'Wish you were here.'

William was always inviting Mr Cleghorn to stay. In the past he'd never wanted to leave the shop, but now he thought – *Why not?* – it would be better than moping about in his flat with nothing to do. He hurried back upstairs, and suddenly the day ahead was no longer empty.

First he wrote to his cousin, accepting the invitation. Then he bought a stamp at the Post Office and posted the letter. Then he got his travelling bag down from the top of the wardrobe and tried to think what to pack. And a few days later he was sitting in the train, half excited and half wondering what on earth he'd let himself in for.

To his relief, William met him at the station, together with his ten-year-old son, Tommy, who addressed Mr Cleghorn as Uncle Albert and insisted on carrying his bag. Back at the house they were welcomed by William's wife with a baby in her arms and two little girls who rushed out to greet him with more cries of "Uncle Albert!" and led him into the kitchen, where the table was laid for supper.

He had brought the children presents – coloured pencils and sweets for the little girls and a load of comics for Tommy – and they chatted to him and vied with each other to ask him questions, and it was like being back in the shop when the children came out of school, which had been his favourite time.

Towards the end of the meal, William said, "I'm busy first thing tomorrow, so, Tommy, why don't you take Uncle Albert to see the pup?"

"What pup?" said Mr Cleghorn.

"It's a seal pup," said William. "It's still being fed by its mother, but she leaves it on its own while she goes fishing, and Tommy has been watching it."

Mr Cleghorn said he'd love to see the pup, and so, the next day, dressed in an old pair of William's gumboots and a waterproof jacket, he took it in turns with Tommy to row across the bay.

They did not have to row very far. Half hidden in a small inlet, a sandy rock stuck out of the water, and on it was something white – a pale little seal, sunning itself. At the sound of the oars, it raised its head to look at them with its big dark eyes.

"It knows me," said Tommy, "because I often

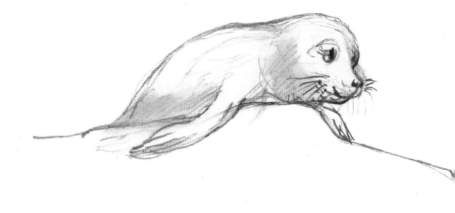

come and see it. Some of the fishermen shoot seals because they say they take their fish, but Pa never does. He says, 'live and let live'." He gazed at it fondly. "Isn't it nice?"

Mr Cleghorn looked at the little seal as it lay contentedly with the sun warming its soft white fur, and thought he had never seen anything so endearing.

After a while he reached for the oars, but Tommy stopped him with a look – and there, a few feet from the rock was the dark, shiny head of a full-grown seal sliding through the water. The little seal sat up and made a noise like a gentle bark. The big seal heaved itself up on the rock and flopped down beside it.

Almost immediately it turned over on its side, and the little seal began happily to suckle.

"It's his mum," whispered Tommy. "I've only ever seen her once before."

They stayed watching a few more moments. Then, very quietly, so as not to disturb them, they rowed back to the shore.

For the rest of the week Mr Cleghorn was swept up into a flood of holiday activities with the family. He helped the children build sandcastles and bought them ice creams, and made them a kite with which they raced all over the beach. Once he went on a fishing expedition with William, which lasted all night. There were picnics and boat rides and sea bathing (though Mr Cleghorn refused to do more than paddle with his trousers hitched up). But he continued to visit the seal pup, sometimes with Tommy and sometimes on his own, and was touched, each time, by its charm and sturdy independence.

Then one morning he found the little pup lying listlessly on its rock. It looked up for a moment at the sound of the oars, but turned its head away at once and lay down again. It seemed sad and thinner than before.

"What's wrong with you, then?" he said. "Hasn't your mum been feeding you?" But he was worried, and when he got back he told William.

William looked serious at once. "When did you last see its mother?" he asked.

"Well, I hardly ever see her," said Mr Cleghorn. "But it's always looked well fed."

"Trouble is," said William, "they were shooting seals up the coast a couple of nights ago. She may have been one of the victims."

"But… but in that case, what will happen to the pup?" said Mr Cleghorn, feeling quite ridiculously upset.

William shook his head. "It can't survive without its mother. Kindest in that case to put it out of its

misery." Then he said, "But let's give it a little longer. She may still turn up."

They went back a day later, Tommy determined that all would be well, Mr Cleghorn apprehensive, and William awkwardly trying to hide his gun in the bottom of the boat.

The pup clearly still hadn't been fed. It was visibly thinner than before, but it was no longer listless. It was angry. At the sight of the boat it sat up and barked – wild, shrill little barks – and slapped its flippers down on the rock.

The sun was still low, but it was going to be a beautiful day and Mr Cleghorn looked at this ridiculous little pale creature in the middle of the shining sea not pleading, but demanding to be fed, to be kept alive in this dazzling world. Out of the corner of his eye, he could see William feeling for his gun, and suddenly he heard himself say something totally absurd.

What Mr Cleghorn said was, "No, don't, William. I'll take it."

He was as surprised as everyone else after he had said it, but when he examined the words he decided that he meant them.

"But you can't," said William. "What on earth would you do with it?" This had also just occurred to Mr Cleghorn, but he thought of the answer just in time.

"I'll give it to the zoo," he said. "There's a little zoo close to where I live. They'll be delighted to have it."

"But how will you get it there?" asked William, increasingly amazed.

Mr Cleghorn glanced at the little seal, now lying down again, but looking, as he thought, directly at him, and was emboldened to say, "By train." He added casually, "I expect it will go in the luggage van."

It was less difficult than Mr Cleghorn had expected to capture the pup. In the end it hardly struggled as William wrapped his coat round it, lifted it off the rock, and lowered it gently into the bottom of the boat. It was almost as though it was glad that something, at last, was happening. As the boat began to move, it gave a little cough of surprise, but then it settled down again and lay quietly watching the moving oars.

The pup was received with mildly shocked surprise by the family. An old tin bath was made into a temporary home for it. The little girls danced round it, singing, "We've got a seal! We've got a seal!" and the baby was brought in wearing only its nappy, to stare at it disapprovingly.

William stirred up some creamy milk, and to the little girls' delight added the remains of a bottle of cod liver oil, a spoonful of which they were normally made to take every morning.

"I'm not sure this will work," he said, and offered a bowlful of the mixture to the seal pup, but it only raised its head, looked at it, and lay down again, so he tilted the bowl in the direction of its face. The pup gave a tremendous sneeze, and a spray of fishy milk flew everywhere.

"It's used to suckling," said Tommy, which gave Mr Cleghorn an idea.

"Could we...?" he said, pointing vaguely. "Do you think...?"

Everyone turned to look at the baby, which was contentedly chewing the top of its empty bottle.

"I'll just try," said Mr Cleghorn. "Excuse me," he said to the baby and pulled the bottle from its clutching fingers. The baby, outraged, screamed, and continued to scream at the top of its voice as, undeterred, Mr Cleghorn quickly filled the bottle with William's mixture.

He made to offer it to the seal pup, but the pup, horrified by the noise, tried to hide in a corner of the tin bath. "I really don't think…" said William. Seeing its bottle being offered to another, the baby's shrieks reached new heights. The little girls blocked their ears, while the baby's mother, clutching it tight to her chest, gave Mr Cleghorn a reproachful look.

"Sorry," said Mr Cleghorn.

But then he had another idea. He suddenly bent down, grabbed the seal pup firmly with both hands and then sat, holding the slippery creature tight to his chest, just as he could see the baby being held by its mother.

The pup struggled wildly, but Mr Cleghorn clung on, getting rather wet in the process, and at last it gave in. As a final protest, it opened its mouth to bark, and Mr Cleghorn cunningly stuck in the bottle. For a moment nothing happened. The seal pup sat unmoving with the teat in its mouth. Then, suddenly, it began to suck. It sucked more and more eagerly until the bottle was empty.

Mr Cleghorn beamed. Then he said, "I think I'll call him Charlie."

"Well, I think you'd better get Charlie to the zoo as soon as possible," said William. "I'm glad he liked my mixture, but he'll need something stronger in the long run. How were you thinking of transporting him?"

By now the pup had drunk two more lots of the mixture and the baby, though still suspicious, had been silenced with another bottle. Mr Cleghorn felt quite calm and efficient.

"If you could spare the tin bath," he said, "it just fits him nicely. And if you could perhaps help me get him to the station?"

In the end it took longer than Mr Cleghorn had hoped to get away. The children insisted on a last picnic on the beach, and there was a last round of ice creams to be bought, and the packing to be done, and a large flagon to be filled with Charlie's mixture for the journey. When they finally set off for the station

with the pup in a small cart pulled by Tommy, it was mid-afternoon.

The pup kept fairly calm during all this. It had clearly accepted the tin bath as its new home and seemed interested rather than bothered when it was moved from one place to another, as long as it could keep Mr Cleghorn in view.

"It thinks you're its mum," said Tommy, as Mr Cleghorn walked beside the cart with the pup's dark eyes fixed earnestly upon him.

The train was already waiting when they got to the station, so William quickly helped Mr Cleghorn load the pup into the luggage van. Mr Cleghorn shook hands with him and hugged the children. Then he climbed aboard, there was a whistle from the engine, the train began to move, everyone waved, and then

Mr Cleghorn was alone in the half-light of the luggage van with a motherless seal pup.

He had expected to spend the journey comfortably settled in his compartment, perhaps checking on the pup every so often, but each time he tried to move away, the pup gave agitated little barks, so finally he sat down on a trunk facing it. As the train rattled through the countryside with dusk falling outside, and he sat there among the luggage with the little seal's eyes upon him, he couldn't help wondering how he had got himself into this position, and exactly what he would do next.

He had always imagined himself taking the seal pup from the station straight to the zoo, where it would be welcomed with grateful cries, and then he would go home. But of course the zoo would be closed. Now the pup would have to come home with him overnight. At once the picture of the janitor rose up before him. Knowing how he felt about small caged birds, what would he say about a large loose seal?

When they finally arrived, it was night. The station appeared deserted, and there was no sign of the cabs that normally waited outside. For a moment Mr Cleghorn was flummoxed, but then he saw some luggage trolleys parked in a corner. "It's all right, Charlie," he said to the pup, "we'll walk."

The pup gave a few questioning coughs as Mr Cleghorn loaded its tin bath on the trolley, steadying it with his travelling bag, but it soon relaxed.

There was almost no one about, and they trundled along the empty streets, with the pup gazing up in wonder at each street lamp as they passed under it.

Mr Cleghorn, meanwhile, tried to think how he would explain the situation to the janitor. "Yes," he tried saying airily, "I have this seal staying with me for the night." But somehow he could not imagine the janitor smiling a welcome.

When they arrived at the house he went in alone to prepare the ground, but to his surprise the hall was empty. He looked inside the janitor's cubbyhole. Empty too. Well, he thought, even janitors had to sleep sometime. But just in case… He quickly fished out one of his shirts from his travelling bag, wrapped the pup in it, and then, as fast as he could, staggered with it across the hall.

The stairs were more difficult, but he struggled up them, with the pup giving a little surprised cough at each step. At one time he thought he heard a door close somewhere, but no one appeared. He unlocked the door of his flat, almost fell inside, staggered to the bathroom, and carefully lowered the pup into the bathtub. Then he collapsed on to the lavatory seat. He'd done it! He'd rescued the pup and got it safely home. And tomorrow he would take it to the zoo.

After collecting his travelling bag, he gave the pup some more of William's mixture. It seemed pleased with the extra space in the bath, and only became agitated again when he tried to leave the bathroom. But he hit on the idea of turning on the tap to a thin trickle, and the pup was so fascinated watching the drops of water falling and disappearing down the plughole that it allowed him to go without complaint.

He was almost too tired to get undressed before he fell into bed, and went immediately to sleep. After a while he began to dream.

He dreamt about trains and boats and the sea. The sea was rough and there were big waves crashing against the rocks, and Mr Cleghorn was trying to hold on to the baby's bottle, but the waves got bigger and bigger and bigger, and the crashes became louder and louder and louder… and suddenly he woke up.

At first he couldn't think where he was. Then he remembered the pup. He looked at his watch. It was half past four in the morning. And there was someone knocking on his door. Why were they knocking on his door at half past four in the morning? Confusedly, he thought of the janitor. Somehow he must have found out about the pup and had come to confront him.

He climbed out of bed and reluctantly opened the door. But it was not the janitor. It was a lady. It was the lady with the birdcage. She was wearing a coat over her nightdress and she shouted, "There is water coming through my ceiling."

"What?" said Mr Cleghorn, but the lady pushed past him, shouting, "I can hear it."

She flung open the bathroom door and revealed the floor running with water. There was more water splashing down from the overflowing bath, and sitting on the bathmat was a bemused looking seal.

"There, you see!" shouted the lady. Then she said, "Oh."

Mr Cleghorn rushed to turn off the tap and plunged his arm down into the water. Somehow the plug had wedged itself back into the plughole. He pulled it out, and the water began to run away.

He started to say, "It was the plug…" but the lady said, "Why have you got a seal in your bathroom?"

Mr Cleghorn said, "I'm taking it to the zoo," and, as the lady still looked puzzled, "They were going to shoot it."

"Ah," said the lady, who had become calmer at the sight of the pup. Mr Cleghorn had found some towels and began quickly to mop up the water. "I'm sorry," he said. "I'll just dry this and then I'll come and look at your ceiling." He noticed that the bath had emptied itself and carefully lifted the pup back into it.

"It's very tame," said the lady.

"It thinks I'm its mother," said Mr Cleghorn. "At least, that's what my cousin's boy told me."

"It probably does if you've been feeding it," said the lady. Then she giggled. "Does the janitor know it's here?"

"Certainly not," said Mr Cleghorn.

"Well, I won't tell him," said the lady. "I'll see you downstairs."

Mr Cleghorn quickly finished wiping the floor and gave the pup a face flannel to play with while he got dressed. Then he went downstairs to the lady's flat. She had drawn back the curtains, and Mr Cleghorn saw that it was no longer quite dark outside. She had also swapped her coat and nightdress for a skirt and blouse.

"Actually, it's not too bad," she said, leading the way to her kitchen. "There's nothing coming through any more."

She pointed to a bucket half-full of water, but the drips had in fact stopped. Mr Cleghorn had a good look round. After all, the only damage seemed to be a small patch of damp on the ceiling.

"I'll soon put a spot of paint on that," he said.
"I'm only sorry I caused you this trouble."

"Well," said the lady, "it was quite an adventure.
It's not every day you meet a harbour seal pup in

the bath." She had put on the kettle and was fussing round the kitchen. "I'm going to make breakfast. Will you have some?"

Mr Cleghorn suddenly realised that he was hungry and said that he would.

As he started on his bacon and eggs, he asked, "How do you know so much about seals?"

"My father was a vet," said the lady. "Only cats and dogs, mostly, but he had a lot of books. When are the zoo people coming to collect your little fellow?"

"The zoo people?" said Mr Cleghorn. "Oh, they're not coming here. I'm taking it to them. They'll be pleased, I think, don't you?"

"You mean they don't know that it's coming?" exclaimed the lady. "But they need to prepare for it. You have to tell them." And as Mr Cleghorn looked taken aback, she added, "I'll come with you, if you like. My father used to know the head keeper – he may still be there. We'll tell them that you are giving them a seal pup and then they can make arrangements." She thought for a moment. "They won't be open for a while yet, but why don't we meet in the hall at nine o'clock?"

"If you're sure," said Mr Cleghorn.

"Quite sure," said the lady. "By the way," she added, "my name is Miss Craig. Miss Millicent Craig."

"Albert Cleghorn," said Mr Cleghorn with a little bow.

"It's quite a long time since I've been there," said Miss Craig later that morning, as they sat on the tram that would take them to the zoo. "But it was always very popular and the animals were well looked after."

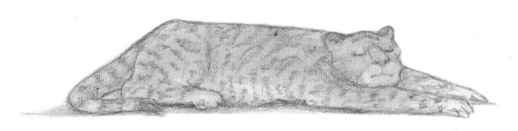

However, there were not many people about when they got there. The animals seemed quiet, too. The elephant was lying down apparently asleep, and there was almost no noise from the monkey house, except when a fight broke out over a bit of food.

Miss Craig was pleased to find that James, the head keeper who had known her father, was still in the job, and he was delighted to see them. It was only when they told him about the seal pup that he became thoughtful.

"I'll take it, of course and do my best for it," he said, "but things are not the same since the accident."

It turned out that the long-time owner of the zoo
had been killed by a fall from the giraffe house, which
he had been inspecting for repairs, and the zoo had
passed to a couple who had no interest in it.

"They never come near it," said the head keeper.
"They've sacked half the staff, and the money is
always late. This week again I've had to pay some of

the bills out of my own pocket. I'd leave, only what would the animals do without me? But don't worry, I'll do my very best for your seal pup."

They walked past the seal pond on their way back. There were two seals lying unmoving on the slightly dirty sand that surrounded it, and there were some sweet-papers floating on the water. Mr Cleghorn said nothing until they had gone out through the gate. Then he said, "I'm not sending Charlie to that place."

There was no tram in view, and Miss Craig said, "Let's walk a little."

A lane led past some cottages to a neglected park, and they found a patch of grass surrounded by trees, with a wooden bench.

"Let's think this out," said Miss Craig. "I agree with you, but what are the alternatives?"

"There must be other zoos," said Mr Cleghorn.

"I don't think there are any near here," said Miss Craig. "My father used to know them all. And of course a lot of them don't even keep seals."

"What about aquariums?"

Miss Craig shook her head regretfully. "Perhaps, after all, this place might not be too bad," she said, but without much conviction. "I'm sure James would do his best for him, and you could visit."

"No," said Mr Cleghorn. Then he said, "Of course I could just keep him."

Miss Craig stared at him.
"Where?" she asked. "You
mean in your flat?"

"It's got a balcony," said Mr Cleghorn quite belligerently. "And I could let him have turns in the bath."

"But dear Mr Cleghorn," said Miss Craig, "seals grow large in no time. He would soon be too big for you to handle."

"Well, just for a while, then," said Mr Cleghorn. "Until we think of something."

"What about his food?" said Miss Craig. "It needs to be just right. I read about it in one of my father's books."

"Well, there might also be information in his books about zoos," said Mr Cleghorn. "There may be some you hadn't heard about, or which have only recently opened."

"I suppose I could write around a bit," said Miss Craig. Then she clapped her hands to her mouth and said, "Oh."

"What is it?" said Mr Cleghorn.

"The janitor," said Miss Craig.

"What about the janitor? There is no reason," said Mr Cleghorn rather grandly, "why the janitor should become aware of Charlie's existence. He didn't see me bring him in, and I don't propose to inform him." He stumbled a little. "If you would help me... You know so much about animals... I'm sure, if you would help me, we could manage it together."

"Well, it would be nice if we could make Charlie happy," said Miss Craig. Suddenly she became very brisk. "All right," she said. "The first thing we have to do is to get him some proper food. And I'd better come and have a look at your balcony. And we should see what else we can find out about seals from those books," she laughed. "What *would* the janitor say?"

They went on sitting in the sun a little longer. Then Miss Craig said, "Right. Next stop is the fish shop," and they set off together to buy Charlie some food.

They found the little pup clearly hungry and giving anxious little coughs, but he brightened up at the sight of Mr Cleghorn. At first he was puzzled by the mixture of milk, fish oil and finely crushed fish that Miss Craig had produced for him, but then he suddenly got the idea and drank it straight from the jug.

"Well, that's his diet settled," said Miss Craig. "He must have been nearly weaned. I'll bring him up another feed this evening."

"In that case," said Mr Cleghorn, "will you stay and have a little supper with me?"

Miss Craig said that she would be delighted, and he spent the afternoon trying to decide between smoked salmon and ham as part of a picnic that he would serve on his balcony.

The balcony had a smooth stone floor and, while he was making his preparations, Mr Cleghorn tried putting Charlie down on it. The little pup

sat, looking thoughtful for a little while, but then he began cautiously to explore, lolloping about on his newly-fed belly. By the time Miss Craig brought him his next meal, he was so at home there that Mr Cleghorn did not have to hold him to feed him, but just offered him the jug where he was.

*

The picnic on the balcony was a success. Mr Cleghorn had finally decided on smoked salmon, and it turned out that this was Miss Craig's favourite food. They ate and talked. Mr Cleghorn talked about his shop, how much he'd enjoyed the running of it and how much he missed it, and Miss Craig talked about her father and the various animals she had sometimes helped him to treat.

They went on talking as the light faded and it gradually became dark, and they were still talking when they could no longer see the pup but could only hear him gently humping about at their feet. In time the movements stopped, and when the moon got up, it showed him stretched out by the railings, fast asleep.

They stood admiring him. "Can we leave him there for the night?" said Mr Cleghorn. "Or do you think they'll be able to see him from the street when it gets light?"

"Hardly," said Miss Craig, "but perhaps you should get some flowers to put round the railings, just in case."

"Perhaps we could choose them together," said Mr Cleghorn.

Miss Craig went a little pink and said, "Of course." Then she exclaimed, "Goodness, I had no idea that it was so late!" and Mr Cleghorn said, "Till tomorrow, then," and saw her to the door.

He cleared away the dishes and was getting ready for bed, when there was a sound from the balcony. He went to look. Outside the balcony door he could see the pup, sitting upright with his face pressed against the glass. He was banging on it with his flippers and giving anxious barks. Mr Cleghorn said "Shush!" and let him in. Charlie waddled quickly inside and lay down at his feet. "What's this then?" said Mr Cleghorn.

"Did you miss your mum?" Charlie said nothing, but looked at him and then closed his eyes. "Sweet dreams," said Mr Cleghorn, as he stepped over him to get into bed, and soon they were both fast asleep.

Next day, Mr Cleghorn and Miss Craig bought four large potted hydrangeas and a watering can. The janitor met them on their way through the hall.

"Going in for horticulture, are we now, Miss Craig?" he said. "Much better than animals. Plants don't rush about and make a noise."

"Miss Craig is going to beautify my balcony," said Mr Cleghorn.

"I'm all for a bit of beauty myself," said the janitor. "Just so long as it isn't creatures."

The plants not only blocked most of the view from below, but looked very pretty. Miss Craig watered them with the new watering can, and then Mr Cleghorn watered Charlie, who rolled about in the spray with little whoops of delight.

Later that day Miss Craig looked through her father's books and wrote to some of his old friends for information about zoos. "I'm sure we'll find someone to take him," she said. "It may just take a little time."

During the next few days, while they waited for replies to her letters, they fed Charlie and played with him on Mr Cleghorn's balcony and let him splash about in Mr Cleghorn's bathtub. Since he had been so ready to slurp his food instead of suckling, Miss Craig tried him with a few very small whole fish in his mixture, and was delighted to find that the pup gobbled them down. After a while, feeding Charlie fish became a game. Mr Cleghorn threw them to him and Charlie tried to catch them before he swallowed them.

The janitor could hardly miss the quantities of fish being carried past his cubbyhole every day, but Mr Cleghorn told him that his doctor had put him on a diet and that Miss Craig had decided to try it also, and the janitor said one did hear it said that fish could be very beneficial.

Charlie thrived, but the first replies to Miss Craig's letters were discouraging. Three small zoos either did not keep seals or did not need any more of them. However, she had hopes of the last, a big zoo in Brighton which had a reputation for excellence.

"Anyway," said Mr Cleghorn, as they were eating their supper together, which had somehow become a habit, "there's no rush."

One evening about a week later they were sitting on Mr Cleghorn's balcony. The plants had been watered and so had Charlie. Charlie's mixture was cooling in its bowl and Mr Cleghorn was throwing him fish,

while Miss Craig was idly watching the street below. When she saw the postman, she said, "I'll just see if there's a letter."

A few minutes later she was back. "From Brighton," she said, waving the envelope. "Do you want to open it?"

It was just unlucky that, as she hurried across to Mr Cleghorn, she should have slipped on the wet floor and skidded into Charlie, who was about to make a rather skilful catch. As a result, the catch turned into a header and the fish shot over the railings and out into the unknown.

Charlie humped over to the railings, giving loud, distressed barks, and on his way knocked over the bowl of his mixture, some of which followed the fish. There was a faint cry from below, then silence.

After a moment Mr Cleghorn peered cautiously over the railings. There was a woman in the street below who appeared to be trying to brush herself down. She glanced up at the balcony and Mr Cleghorn quickly ducked.

When he looked again, she seemed about to move on, and for a moment it seemed as though everything might still be all right. But then an elderly couple approached. The woman turned to speak to them, and they all looked up at the balcony. A few angry words floated up to Mr Cleghorn. Then a delivery boy and a man with a briefcase joined them. The angry talk grew louder, and then the front door of the house opened and the janitor emerged.

"He'll come up here," said Mr Cleghorn. "We'd better be ready for him. Come on, Charlie." He quickly threw down the remaining fish in front of the bemused pup, hustled Miss Craig inside and closed the balcony door.

When the janitor appeared, they met him in the hall.

"I'm so dreadfully sorry," said Mr Cleghorn, before the janitor could say anything. "Our lunch… so clumsy… how is the poor lady? We'll come downstairs with you now to speak to her," and the janitor seemed about to agree, when there came the sound of several sharp barks from the balcony.

The janitor froze. "That's a dog," he said. "You've got a dog in there. I'm not having dogs secretly secreted in my house!" and he pushed past them into the living room, to be confronted by Charlie upright outside the balcony door, barking and banging on the glass with his flippers.

After this all was lost. The janitor was beside himself. "Not even a dog!" he yelled, "but some slimy, wet..." Words failed him and he could only stammer, "Out! Out!"

Mr Cleghorn had to promise that the pup would be gone first thing in the morning and eventually he and Miss Craig were left on the balcony trying to calm Charlie and to think what on earth to do with him.

Miss Craig had kept the letter from Brighton in her hand all through the upheaval. "This may yet solve everything," she said, and opened it. But even as she unfolded it, she somehow knew that it would be bad news. "They're in the process of redesigning all their water accommodation," she said. "They can't have him."

"So..." said Mr Cleghorn. Miss Craig nodded. Neither of them wanted to put it into words. "There's no other choice," she said.

✳

They spent a miserable evening making arrangements. They could hardly take Charlie to the zoo on the tram, but Mr Cleghorn found that the luggage trolley, which he had never got round to returning, was still parked at the back of the flats where he had left it. Miss Craig packed up a quantity of Charlie's mixture and some of his fish to take with him.

"It will help him over the first few days," she said.

"And I can stay with him for a while and make sure that they give it to him," said Mr Cleghorn.

Then they both said, "It may not be so bad," but neither of them believed it.

*

They made an early start in the morning. The janitor, exhausted by the emotions of the previous day, was not yet on duty as Mr Cleghorn quickly carried Charlie through the hall and out through the front door. Charlie protested mildly at being put into the tin bath, which was a rather tighter fit than before, and looked questioningly at Mr Cleghorn when it was loaded on to the luggage trolley. However, once Mr Cleghorn started pushing it along the road with Miss Craig walking beside it, he gazed round quite happily, giving little barks of surprise at the passing trams and carts.

They arrived at the zoo before opening time, so they pushed the trolley up the lane to the park and sat down to wait on the bench, where, not long before, they had made such brave plans for Charlie. After a moment Mr Cleghorn could stand it no longer and said, "Let's give Charlie one last game."

Charlie was so happy darting and diving for his fish in the grass that Mr Cleghorn did not have the heart to put an end to it, and by the time he finally lifted him back into the tin bath, opening time was long past. "All right," he said, "let's get on with it."

Miss Craig said, "All right," with equal determination, and they marched back to the zoo.

However, the entrance was still closed. There was a chain with a lock dangling on the gate; the glassed-in ticket office was empty, and there was nobody at all about.

"It's not a bank holiday, is it?" said Miss Craig.

Mr Cleghorn checked in his diary, but it wasn't.

A sign on the wall clearly listed the opening 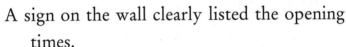 times.

The zoo should definitely be open. They could hear the faint trumpeting of an elephant in the distance, otherwise everything was quiet.

"What on earth do we do now?" said Mr Cleghorn. But Miss Craig said, "Look."

Inside the zoo, two men were approaching the gate. One was wearing a dark suit and the other seemed to be one of the keepers. The keeper unlocked the gate, and as he came out, the man in the suit said, "I'm sorry," and Mr Cleghorn recognised the bank manager. The keeper nodded and was about to lock the gate again, but Miss Craig intercepted him. "Please," she said. "What's happening? We've come to see James."

"It was you about the seal pup the other day, wasn't it?" said the keeper. "I'm afraid James won't be able to help you now." He smiled grimly. "Oh, come in anyway. You may be able to cheer him up." Then he hurried away, saying, "Excuse me, but I have to see to the potentials."

"What on earth are the potentials?" said Miss Craig.

"I've got an awful feeling I can guess," said Mr Cleghorn. They pushed the trolley along,

with Charlie remarking on the various animals with
astonished little barks. Outside the elephant house
a man was looking at the elephants and making
notes in a little book. There were two more men
outside the lions' cage. As they passed them,
one of them turned to look at Charlie and said,
"What about this one? He looks nice and lively!"
and seemed about to address Mr Cleghorn, who
pushed past him quickly without speaking.

They found James in his office surrounded by papers and with his head in his hands, but before he could speak, Mr Cleghorn said, "Don't tell me. Your owners have done a flit."

James sat up so quickly that some of the papers fell on the floor and said, "How did you know?"

"I'm a businessman," said Mr Cleghorn. "I know what can happen in business."

"They've taken everything," said James. "Every

penny. We have to sell the animals. There are potential buyers out there now. Some of them are from a circus – I don't know how they got to hear about it. But a circus! The terrible thing is that any animals we can't find homes for will have to be put down. And all because of a pair of stupid, greedy, dishonest... How can people do such things?"

"That's terrible," said Miss Craig. "I expect you've tried the bank?"

"The bank manager tried," said James. "We all tried. Some of the keepers even offered their savings. But a place like this needs a proper large investment. We can't get anywhere near that." Then he began to talk about all the plans he had made with the previous owner. "We were going to enlarge," he said. "With a special water display – you know, like they're going to have in Brighton. And a separate children's zoo. And we'd almost got the money, too. The silly thing is that this was a successful business before they came."

He was interrupted by a crash followed by a yelp, and Miss Craig exclaimed, "Charlie!" They found him on the ground with the tin bath on its side, having somehow manoeuvred it off the trolley.

The two men who had noticed him before were standing nearby, having clearly observed him, and one of them laughed and said, "He's an acrobat as well!"

When Charlie saw Mr Cleghorn he lolloped quickly towards him and tried to sit on his shoe. Mr Cleghorn glared at the men. Then he carried the pup inside, where Miss Craig pacified him with some of his mixture and James checked that

he wasn't hurt.

For a while they sat in silence. Miss Craig spotted a kettle in a corner and said, "Perhaps we should have some tea," and helped James make it.

Mr Cleghorn sat deep in thought, absent-mindedly watching Charlie, who was investigating a piece of paper on the floor with his flipper. Finally he said, "Well, my problem just now is that this chap needs a home."

"I know," said James. "I wish I could help."

Mr Cleghorn stood up and walked over to the table. Then he said, "You may be able to. Shall we have a look at these figures?"

James's face changed. "Really?" he said.

"I've run a shop for years," said Mr Cleghorn. "They paid me a fortune for it, and I like running things. A zoo can't be that different." He picked up one of the sheets. "Let's see what we find."

Miss Craig looked from one to the other. Then she retrieved the piece of paper (which turned out to be a bill for camel fodder) from Charlie, and announced that she was going for a walk.

When she came back an hour later, Charlie was asleep in a corner and there were even more papers on the floor. Mr Cleghorn and James had their heads together and were saying things like "have to look into it" and "I don't see why not." So she went for another walk.

On her way back she observed
the potential buyers being
led to the gate by one of the
keepers. They looked rather
cross. But inside the office
Mr Cleghorn and James were
beaming and Mr Cleghorn
said, "Solved. We've got a
zoo."

The keepers were called in to be told that the
zoo was saved. Mr Cleghorn was introduced as
the new owner. He explained that James would be
running it as before and that those
keepers who had been dismissed
would be brought back, so the
animals could once again be
properly looked after. He was
sure that once everything was
back to normal the visitors
would flock back, and that
it would then be possible to
implement James's plans for
expansion.

There were cries of approval and cheers. Everybody wanted to shake Mr Cleghorn's hand, while Miss Craig watched and smiled.

"Will you be living on the premises?" asked the keeper who had opened the gate for them. It turned out that all previous owners except the last couple had lived in a cottage behind the office. "It's very comfortable," he said. "I could show Mrs Cleghorn if she likes."

Miss Craig went a little pink. "Oh," she said, "Mr Cleghorn and I are not married."

At this, a strange feeling came over Mr Cleghorn. It was like the time in the boat when he had first adopted Charlie. He heard himself saying something absurd, but knew as soon as he'd said it that he meant it. What he said this time was, "But perhaps we could be." Then he went pink too.

He and Miss Craig looked at each other. Then Miss Craig said, "Let's walk a little."

Later, the boy whose job it was to sweep behind the cages reported that Mr Cleghorn had gone down on one knee to Miss Craig outside the small cats' house, and that afterwards they had stood very close together for a quite considerable time.

The wedding reception was held next to the seal pond, where the new water display would later be built.

It turned out that the two resident seals were both middle-aged females who vied with each other to mother Charlie, and Mr Cleghorn came several times a day to throw them fish.

Under Mr Cleghorn's management and with advice from his wife, the new zoo became a great success, even rivalling the one in Brighton. It was known especially for its seals and sea lions who had an unusual amount of freedom and played games with their keepers.

Mr Cleghorn's cousin William and his family often came to visit, and a few years later Tommy, who had first discovered Charlie and had never lost his affection for seals, became a keeper himself, eventually taking over from James.

And...

...they all lived happily...

...ever after!

AFTERWORD

Alfred Kerr
Grunewald 1927.

When I was a small girl in Berlin, there was a room in our house called the red room, which my mother had lovingly furnished as a study for my writer father. However, he preferred to work on a wooden table in his bedroom, where the floor was permanently covered in papers, and the red room became a place mainly for visitors.

Apart from the handsome unused desk and matching chair, the room also contained various objects my father had brought back from his travels, and among them was a small stuffed seal which sat contentedly on the polished floor. I was always very pleased when the room was in use, because then I got to see the seal, and I used to sit on it and stroke its fur.

Stuffed animals were not particularly rare in those days before photography had taken hold. People quite often had their pets stuffed, as a way of preserving their memory, but a seal was unusual. When I asked my father about it, he told me that it had once lived on his balcony. It was only much later, when we were refugees in England and long after the little seal, along with the rest of our possessions, had been confiscated by the Nazis, that he told me the rest of the story.

More than a hundred years ago, when my father was a young man, he was staying in Normandy with a fisherman's family, and one day he went out with the fisherman in his boat. The fisherman was shooting seals because they were taking too many of the fish which were his livelihood, but he chose the victims carefully, and so he was quite upset when he found that he had accidentally shot a female with a pup. This meant that he would have to shoot the pup as well, because without its mother it would slowly starve to death. But my father, who loved animals, said no, he would take it and look after it.

So the little seal was put on some seaweed in a box, and it made the long journey to Berlin in the luggage van, where my father visited it regularly to trickle water over it and to try, not very successfully, to feed it a mixture of milk and cod liver oil. By the time they arrived in Berlin late at night, my father had used up all the milk, so he and the pup took a taxi to a restaurant, where my father ordered more milk for it, presumably to the other diners' surprise. Then they were driven back to his flat, where my father put it first in the bath and then on his balcony.

By this time the little seal had become attached to my father and it tried to follow him with little cries of complaint when he went back inside. From then on it always wanted to be with him, and in the following days, whenever it saw my father inside the room, would demand to be let in by leaning up against the balcony door and banging on the glass with its flippers. Then my father would either let it in or he would go out and try to comfort it by trickling water over it with a watering can. He must have hoped to keep it at least until it grew too big. The German for seal is Seehund, which translates as sea dog, and my father told me that the Eskimos often kept them as pets, as we keep dogs.

However, the pup was far from being weaned and, whatever he tried, my father could not feed it enough. At one time he soaked an old jacket in the milky mixture and the pup managed to suck some of it up, but it was not enough, and in any case it was not nearly as nourishing as its mother's milk.

When this became clear, my father asked the Berlin zoo to take it, but for some reason they were unable to, and the Berlin aquarium couldn't take it either. He watched the little creature getting thinner and sadder and in the end there was nothing to be done but to have it put down. And later, stuffed, to be fondly remembered.

I always loved this story. I wished I could have known the little seal, and I wished more than anything that the story could have had a happy ending. Perhaps that is why, more than a hundred years later, I have made up a very different story, which has one.